CHARLIE
Plays Ball

To my sports-playing, ball-throwing,
fun-loving family. Life with you is a blast!
Love, Mama

Charlie Plays Ball
Text copyright © 2015 by Ree Drummond
Illustrations copyright © 2015 by Diane deGroat
All rights reserved. Printed in the United States of America.
No part of this book may be used or reproduced in any manner whatsoever
without written permission except in the case of brief quotations embodied in
critical articles and reviews. For information address HarperCollins Children's Books,
a division of HarperCollins Publishers, 195 Broadway, New York, NY 10007.
www.harpercollinschildrens.com

Library of Congress Cataloging-in-Publication Data
Drummond, Ree.
Charlie plays ball / by Ree Drummond ; illustrations by Diane deGroat. — First edition.
pages cm
Summary: "Charlie the basset hound participates in a variety of sports on the ranch"—
Provided by publisher.
ISBN 978-0-06-229752-5 (hardback)
[1. Basset hound—Fiction. 2. Dogs—Fiction. 3. Ranch life—Fiction. 4. Sports—Fiction.]
I. deGroat, Diane, illustrator. II. Title.
PZ7.D8277Cgs 2015   2014026692   [E]—dc23   CIP   AC

The artist used Winsor & Newton watercolor paint over digital art on
140 lb. Arches hot-press paper to create the illustrations for this book.
Typography by Rachel Zegar
15 16 17 18 19 PC 10 9 8 7 6 5 4 3 2 1
❖
First Edition

CHARLIE
Plays Ball

by Ree Drummond

illustrations by Diane deGroat

HARPER
An Imprint of HarperCollinsPublishers

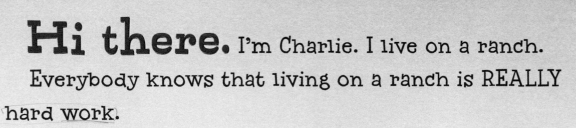

Hi there. I'm Charlie. I live on a ranch. Everybody knows that living on a ranch is REALLY hard work.

Especially for ranch dogs like *me*.

There's lots of riding . . .

roping . . .

feeding . . .

fixing . . .

and making sure pesky critters stay away
from our homestead!

I'm also very good at eating.
Mama says I'm so good at eating, she doesn't
know if she'll ever have enough food!

I just tell her I'm a hardworking ranch dog.
And hardworking ranch dogs have to EAT.

Yep, we work hard on the ranch. But we play hard, too! There's always time for that.

We climb big mountains . . .

swim with curious creatures . . .

explore new territories . . .

leap tall hay bales in a single bound . . .

and boy, oh boy, oh *boy* . . . do we *love* to play **ball!**
Playing ball is *very* big around here.

My favorite ball is
FOOTBALL.

I guess you could say
football is my life.

First, Daddy throws the football.
Then everyone goes crazy!
Todd loves to tackle Bryce.

Hmm. Bryce dropped the ball.

Sniff sniff. Does that mean it's mine?

Ahhh.

That's much better.

Oh, good. **Snacks!**

Narmph . . . yumph . . . numph . . .

Yep. Football's my favorite, all right.

But wait. Soccer!

Playing soccer is so much fun.

Whew. This sure is a lot of running around!

Hmmm . . . I think I'd better lie down for a minute.

This looks like a comfy spot!

Snort—HUH?!? What'd I miss?

What's that bounce-bounce-bouncing noise?

Now we're talking. **Basketball!**
I love basketball. And Mama
loves it, too!
They sure are good at this!

Wow. They're too fast for me!

There goes Mama. . . .

She shoots . . .
She scores!

She rubs my ears.

Ahhh . . .

Basketball . . .

soccer ball . . .

football . . .

DINNERTIME!

Hooray!

My very favorite ball of all!

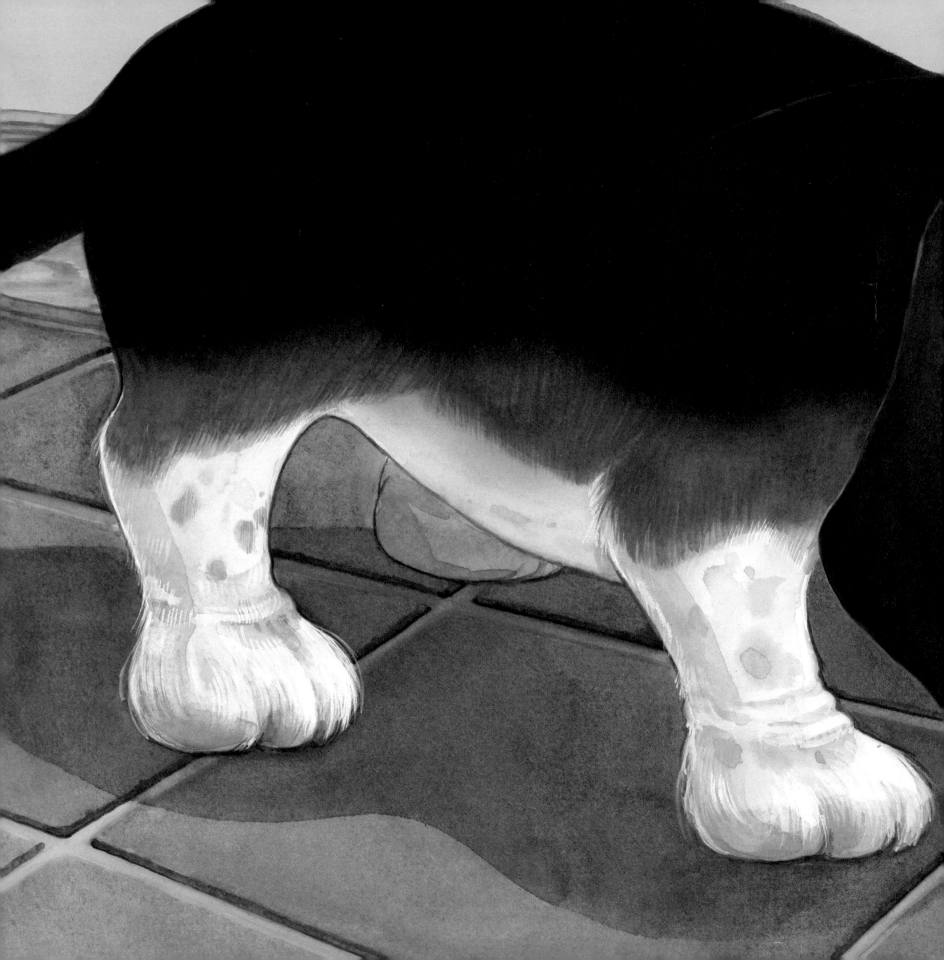

Charlie's Favorite Spaghetti and Meatballs

Makes 8 servings

Be safe! Always cook with an adult. Don't touch sharp knives or hot stoves and ovens! And always wash your hands before and after cooking.

Meatball Ingredients

1½ pounds ground beef
2 cloves garlic, minced
¾ cup bread crumbs
½ cup freshly grated Parmesan
2 eggs
¼ teaspoon salt
Freshly ground black pepper
¼ cup flat-leaf parsley, minced
Splash of milk
¼ cup olive oil

Sauce Ingredients

1 onion, diced
2 cloves garlic, minced
1 28-ounce can whole tomatoes
1 28-ounce can crushed tomatoes
¼ teaspoon salt
Freshly ground black pepper
1 tablespoon sugar
¼ cup flat-leaf parsley, minced
8 whole fresh basil leaves, cut
    into slivers (optional)

2 pounds spaghetti, cooked according
to the package directions
Extra Parmesan, for sprinkling

Instructions

1. To make the meatballs, combine meat, garlic, bread crumbs, Parmesan, eggs, salt, pepper, parsley, and a splash of milk in a mixing bowl. Mix together well. Roll into 25 1½-inch balls and place on a cookie sheet. Place cookie sheet in the freezer for 5 to 10 minutes to firm them up.

2. To brown the meatballs, heat olive oil in a heavy pot or large skillet over medium-high heat. Add meatballs 8 at a time, turning to brown. Remove and drain on a paper towel after each batch. Set meatballs aside.

3. Now you will start the sauce in the same pot. Add the onion and garlic and cook for a few minutes or until translucent. Pour in whole tomatoes and crushed tomatoes. Add salt, pepper, sugar, and parsley. Stir to combine and cook over medium heat for 20 minutes.

4. Add meatballs to pot and stir in gently. Reduce heat to a simmer and cook for 30 minutes, stirring very gently a couple of times during the simmer.

5. Just before serving, stir in basil if using.

6. Serve over cooked spaghetti. Sprinkle with extra Parmesan.